gudetama's guide to life

text by Brian Elling

Penguin Workshop
An Imprint of Penguin Random House

PENGUIN WORKSHOP
Penguin Young Readers Group
An Imprint of Penguin Random House LLC

All rights reserved. Published in 2018 by Penguin Workshop, an imprint of Penguin Random House LLC, 345 Hudson Street, New York, New York 10014. PENGUIN and PENGUIN WORKSHOP are trademarks of Penguin Books Ltd, and the W colophon is a trademark of Penguin Random House LLC. Manufactured in China.

ISBN 9781524784645   10 9 8 7 6 5 4 3

"life is a do-it-yourself project"
—gudetama

turn the page

**Hi! Welcome to *Gudetama's Guide to Life.*
Your go-to guidebook for living life to the almost fullest!**

Each page of this book is kind of packed with helpful lessons,
inspiring quotes, and helpful advice that will have you lying around
like a lazy egg in no time! And all of it comes straight from the yolk
of a Gudetama! With a little help from me along the way.

So read on! I guarantee, no matter what challenges you face,
a Gudetama has some answer or another!

—Nisetama-san

Finding Your Inner Gudetama

Search deep within! Everyone has a little Gudetama inside them. Especially after breakfast.

I see nothing

still nothing

enlightenment

Physical Anatomy of a Gudetama

Every Gudetama is unique. But they all share some basic parts. Use the chart on the next page to fully understand what it is you're looking at (and trying to be like).

I feel so exposed

Shell: As needed

Eyes: Vacant or at least in mid-thought

Nose: Unnecessary

Yolk: Yellow and jiggly

Mouth: Slightly open, even when sleeping

White: Translucent and removable

Beneath the Shell

Many mysteries lie under the shell of the Gudetama.
Learn them so that you may one day understand them!

I can't snap out of it

While they are extremely charming,
Gudetama (and all eggs) lack spunk!

At times, multiple Gudetama can appear
at once. This is a very lucky sight!

you again?

I feel pretty

Gudetama is neither a boy nor a
girl. Gudetama is gender-neutral.

It's impossible to tell a Gudetama from a regular egg. Don't be embarrassed if you find yourself talking to an egg that doesn't respond. This happens all the time.

I'm not here

Gudetama's favorite food is soy sauce.

where am I?

Once a Gudetama is eaten, it is gone and cannot be replaced. Think about that!

Gudetama
Icebreakers

First impressions are everything! Use these Gudetama icebreakers to help jump-start your next meet-and-greet with an egg.

are you tired?

is it loud in here?

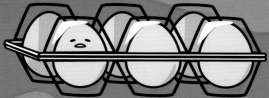

am I right?

say something

leave me alone

identify yourself

do I know you?

go ahead I'm listening

You're One in a Million

Just like no two Gudetama are exactly alike, there are no two people who are exactly alike. So remember, you are as original and beautiful as an egg! Unless you're a clone of someone else.

you're touching me

Follow Your Heart

A Gudetama will always follow their heart, usually to a nap.
They're a perfect role model if you're seeking true happiness.

I don't know the way

Gudetama
Daily Dos

To live like Gudetama, one must do like Gudetama.
To follow the way of the egg, follow these simple rules!

1. do sleep

2. do relax

3. do hide

4. do breathe

5. do sleep again

Gudetama
Daily Don'ts

But remember, the things you don't do are as important as those you do do!

1. don't be afraid

2. don't tempt fate

3. don't hate

4. don't overdo it

5. don't move a lot

too much

My Dream Board

A dream board is a place to write down your greatest wishes!
Using this Gudetama dream board as an example, you too
can be inspired to achieve your dreams! Or at least look at them!

fun...

ugh

shiny

some day...

yes

friends?

no thanks

not today

ehh...

trick or
soy sauce

wish

sleep

The Many Faces of Gudetama

Gudetama are fascinating to watch. You can learn a lot just by watching them sit on your plate for hours and hours. But be careful! Not all Gudetama make good role models. Some have very bad habits!

Basic Gudetama: Most common. Lazy and unenthusiastic.

Raw: The purest egg. Generally easygoing.

Hard-Boiled: Major complainer!

Sliced: Indecisive. Impossible to please.

Egg Tofu: Has a soft side.

Soft-Boiled: Usually has a cold and might be contagious. Avoid!

Quiche: An international Gudetama. Has some attitude. Does not speak English, but understands hand gestures.

Deep-fried egg: Troublesome but fun.

Life Lessons from Nisetama-san

Whenever I'm having a bad day, I shut the door to my room and dance it out! Then I feel better. Try my dance moves the next time you feel low. They work wonders!

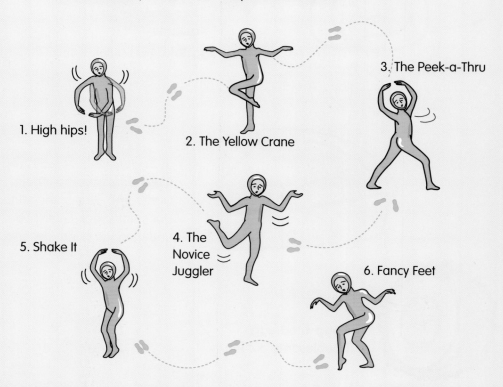

1. High hips!

2. The Yellow Crane

3. The Peek-a-Thru

4. The Novice Juggler

5. Shake It

6. Fancy Feet

Gudetama Dance Moves

Gudetama are no strangers to the dance floor. Wow your friends by rolling out their moves at your next party! And the best part is, you can do them all without getting out of your seat!

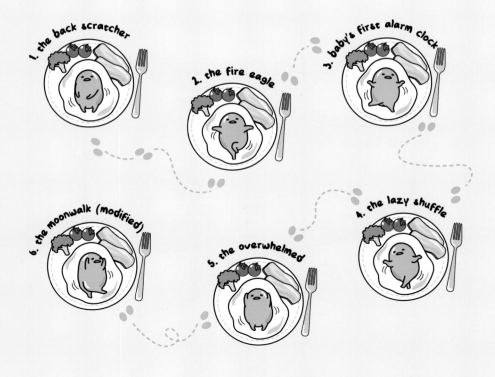

1. the back scratcher
2. the fire eagle
3. baby's first alarm clock
4. the lazy shuffle
5. the overwhelmed
6. the moonwalk (modified)

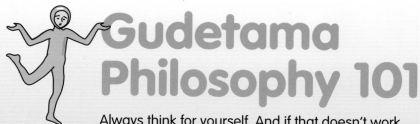

Gudetama Philosophy 101

Always think for yourself. And if that doesn't work, think like a Gudetama.

is anything ever half full?

it's all relative

not today

change is inevitable

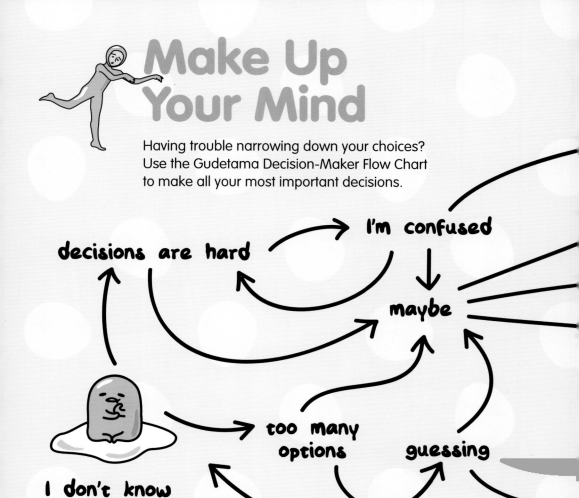

Make Up Your Mind

Having trouble narrowing down your choices?
Use the Gudetama Decision-Maker Flow Chart
to make all your most important decisions.

I'm confused

decisions are hard

maybe

too many options

guessing

I don't know what I want

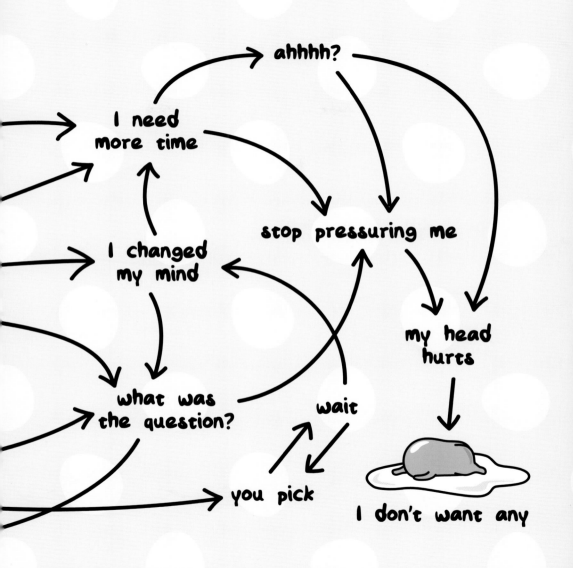

Home Sweet Home

Gudetama like to be comfortable. To make your egg (and you) as cozy as can be, follow these guidelines!

Set the temperature to a comfortable 72 degrees. Never freeze your Gudetama!

why?

I'm sensitive

Provide your Gudetama with a soft place to rest. Any slice of bread or even a layer of rice or mixed greens will do.

Gudetama need entertainment or they get cranky. Keep their minds active!

I'm done

Keep your Gudetama covered. Otherwise they spoil!

this is it?

Keep the space around your Gudetama tidy. They get unhappy when things are messy.

can't think

Gudetama sometimes like to just be left alone.

hello?

Sing Like Nobody's Listening

Be bold, but in a Gudetama way!
Here's an example of an egg in action!

1. sing like nobody's listening

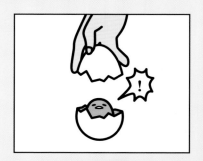

2. until they are

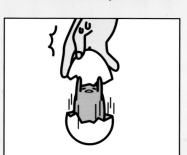

3. then hide

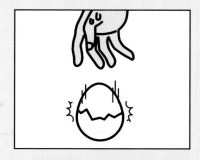

4. and never speak of it again

Get That Gudetama Style

When it comes to fashion, no one has more style than a Gudetama! So go ahead and copy their iconic looks! Eggs don't mind.

feeling patriotic

beach party

old-school

aspen

night on the town

annual book-club brunch

Daily Affirmations

Repeating positive thoughts over and over makes them more likely to come true. Practice these Gudetama mantras to manifest powerful results!

not my problem

not today

I'm tired

choose lazy

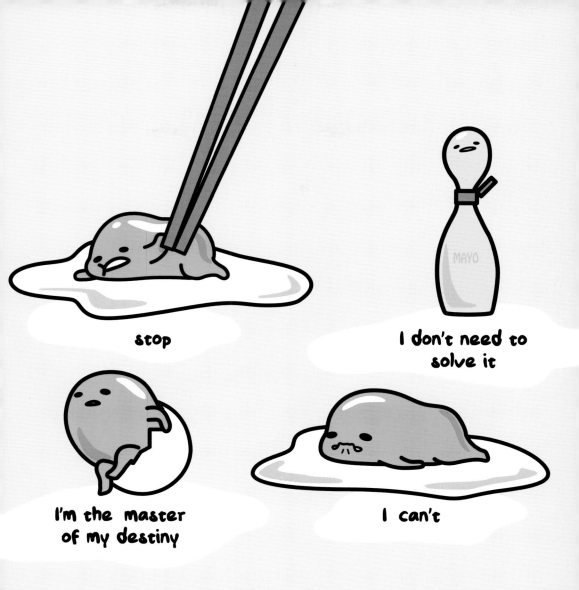

Too Much of a Good Thing

Eggs know how to have a good time . . . and when it's a good time to go home! And you should, too!

You Are
What You Eat

Your Gudetama spends a lot of time with food! That's why eggs know the importance of healthy eating. Here's the Gudetama guide to proper nutrition!

Sushi:
Healthy and light

Pancakes:
Cake without the icing

Soft-boiled egg:
Dainty and delicious

I'm at a loss

honestly?

how
civilized

Ramen noodles:
Hearty food for the soul

Cake:
Adds smiles and inches

Ice cream:
A good thing once
in a while

it's harder
than it looks

you're staring
again

I feel
different

Life Lessons from Nisetama-san

Money matters! But not to a Gudetama! So I put together some advice to keep your mind on your money.

Put your money where your yellow jumpsuit is.

A penny saved is shiny!

Money makes the egg go 'round!

Time is money. That's why watches are so expensive.

How much do you really spend on a rainy day?

Be Open to New Experiences

A true Gudetama is always open to new experiences.
That means keeping yourself raw and ready! You never know
when something sort of okay will come your way.

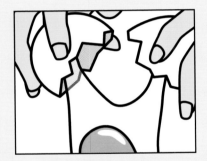

1. ahh, it's cold

2. huh?

3. my face . . .

4. it's over

Gudetama and the Art of Conversation

Gudetama are master conversationalists. Here are some of my recent talks with eggs that have gone really well.

Hello! Nice to meet you. My name is Nisetama-san. What's your name?

hi

Wow! It sure is nice weather we're having. Don't you think?

sure

So, tell me something about yourself?

do you have any soy sauce?

I like long walks on the beach.
Do you like the beach?

Do you like watching movies?

Well, it was nice talking to you.

Do the Right Thing

Every Gudetama knows the difference between right and wrong, even if they don't want to. The next time you have a moral dilemma, think: "What would Gudetama do?"

enjoy soy sauce?

right

take that extra nap?

stay relaxed?

get up early
to view pretty
sunrise?

design plastic
packaging that's
hard to open?

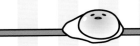

wrong

read self-help book?

Get Fit

Exercise is important for every Gudetama. But getting them up and on their feet can take some coaxing. Here are some exercises that work well for eggs (and humans who want to be like eggs).

Push-Ups

nope

Jumping Jacks

too much

Leg Lifts

are we done yet?

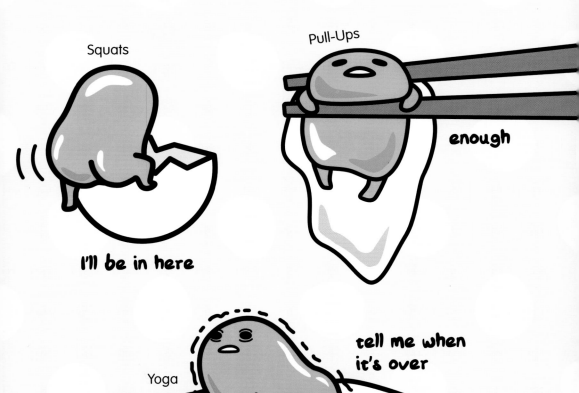

Strategies for Conflict Management

Conflict is unavoidable. People and eggs face it every day.
Follow these steps to get out of any tough situation.

1. stay still

2. pretend to be invisible

3. protect your assets

4. admit defeat

Be Self-Reliant

Every Gudetama knows to look out for numero uno!
So make sure to take care of yourself. Because no one else will.

"me" time

A Lesson in Social Media

If you're going to learn anything from the Gudetama, you have to learn their lingo. Especially when it comes to chatting on social media!

bffn
(best friend for now)

lol
(lying on laptop)

rgtg
(really got to go)

brb
(been really bored)

omg
(oh my gude)

irl
(I'm really lazy)

Be Adaptable

Constant change is a part of life. And the faster you learn that lesson, the happier you'll be. For inspiration, look no further than a Gudetama.

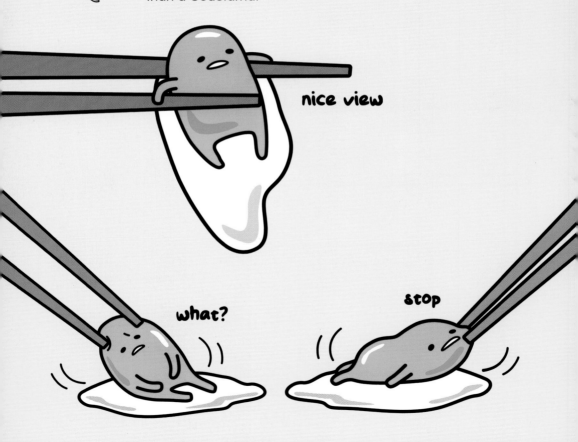

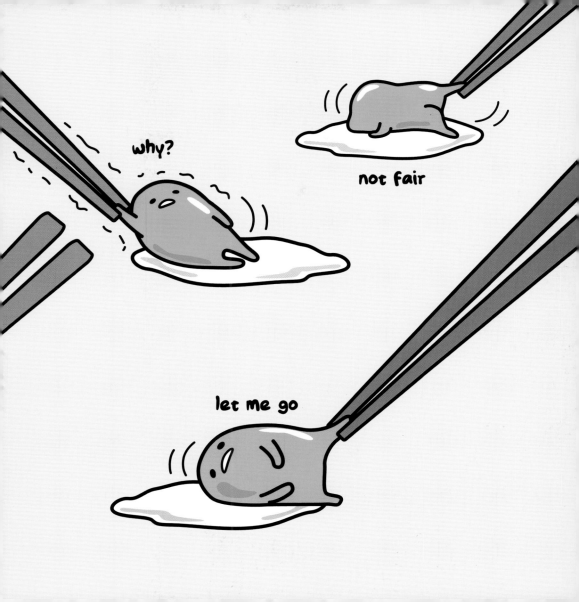

A Moment of Reflection

Whenever a Gudetama gets stressed or uneasy, they take a quiet moment to center their yolk. Try taking a moment for yourself now. Shhh.

that's all

Don't Be So Hard on Yourself

Everyone makes mistakes. Even if you're a Gudetama.
So, next time you mess up, give yourself a break!

born to be soft

How to Get a Gudetama Night's Sleep

No one sleeps better than a Gudetama. Check out how eggs get all those healthy zzzzz's.

step 1: be tired

step 4: curl up

step 2: wait not very long

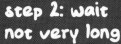

step 3: get more tired

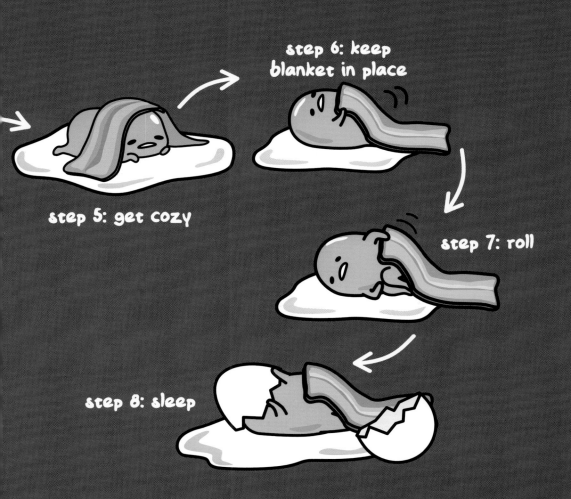

Life Lessons from Nisetama-san

As the number-one fan of Gudetama, I have almost become one (I hope). You can make the same amazing transformation, just by following these three easy steps!

Dress like Gudetama!

Lounge like Gudetama!

Own it!

Go Ahead, Indulge Yourself

All Gudetama know the importance of treating themselves to something special. Any time is a good time to indulge in the things you love.

Manners

Proper manners are essential. Follow the etiquette of the Gudetama and you'll save yourself from serious embarrassment at your next formal dinner!

nope

please

I insist

Keep Under the Radar

A good Gudetama knows when to lie low to stay out of trouble. Don't make a spectacle of yourself if you want to be left alone!

wallflower is
a compliment

Life Isn't a Bowl of Lollipops

Life can be difficult. Once you accept that fact, everything else will be a lot easier to deal with. It's the Gudetama way!

get used to it

 # Speak Your Mind

Gudetama say whatever comes to mind. They're a lesson in putting it out there! Just take a look!

I'm dizzy

sleep is everything

I wish I was kidding

I had too much

no, you're
in a bubble

not now

this feels off

sigh . . .

Winning Isn't Everything

Winning isn't as important as doing your best! Take the sting out of that next temporary setback by following these Gudetama examples!

I can't

I'm not going to pretend

can I go now?

is it over yet?   pass   I give up

Life Lessons from Nisetama-san

If you want to get in good with a Gudetama, do lots of things for them! They love it! And eventually you might, too.

faster

Silence Is Yellow

Remember, you don't have to participate in every conversation. Gudetama know that silence is the best way to maintain control.

Patience Is the Key to Success

Don't let anyone pressure you into doing something you don't want to do! Instead, trust your instinct to do nothing, just like a Gudetama!

wait for it

time-out

I'm tired

five more minutes

maybe later

Gudetama Guide to Skin Care

Proper skin care is essential to maintaining your youthful glow. Have you ever met a Gudetama whose yolk wasn't gleaming? Here's their secret!

Exfoliate.

scratchy

Moisturize daily.

I can't go on like this

Keep those
pores clean!

Limit your exposure
to the sun.

too hot

I'm done

 # Be Zen

Gudetama know that stillness is the path to inner peace.
So try sitting still or maybe take up yoga or join a monastery.

I'm meditating

Just Do Your Part

The Gudetama remind us we are all just cogs in the bigger wheel of life. Release control and you will be free!

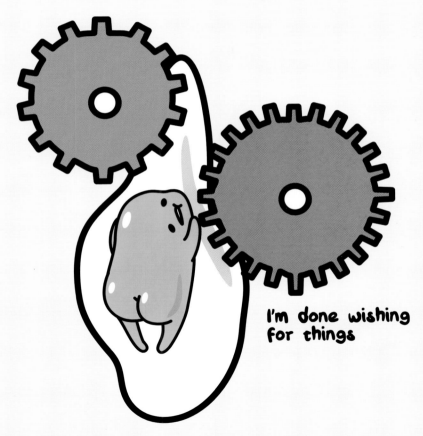

I'm done wishing for things

Keep in Touch

Every Gudetama knows that keeping up with friends and family can be a challenge. But it's important! So take time to remind your loved ones that you care for them. It's worth it!

stamps are hard

please don't pick up

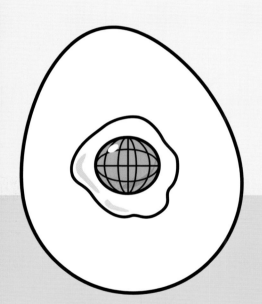

it's in my
junk folder

I'm kind of busy

Eggspect the Uneggspected

A true Gudetama knows that everything can change in a moment!
But they usually aren't paying enough attention to notice.

it is what it is

Smile

Any Gudetama knows that there's nothing more important than keeping a smile on your face! After all, you never know who's watching!

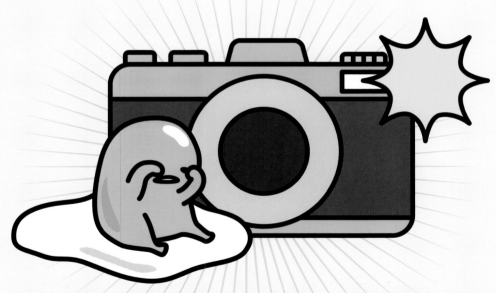

I wasn't ready

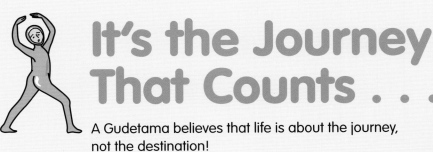

It's the Journey That Counts . . .

A Gudetama believes that life is about the journey, not the destination!

no end in sight

where am I going?

I'm having second thoughts

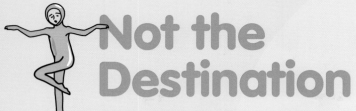

Not the Destination

But no matter what happens along the way, remember to enjoy the ride. Who knows! You may end up somewhere you never expected!

is something burning?

Gratitude Is Everything

We all have things we take for granted in life. So take a moment to look around and appreciate all the good things around you!

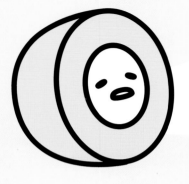

it's more than I imagined

whatever

it just keeps coming

What's the Meaning of Life?

Unfortunately, even the Gudetama don't have any answers to life's biggest question. But I'm sure some egg will figure it out soon. Until then, just have fun and do what you love.

I'm gonna sleep on it